Lawrence

by Janet Morgan Stoeke

DUTTON CHILDREN'S BOOKS

New York

"If I were a *brave* hedgehog," thought Lawrence, "I'd be at the Grand Cafe right now, eating coconut cream pie."

Lawrence loved coconut cream pie. But to get it, he'd have to go to the Grand Cafe.

It was a scary place, with enormous waiters and trouble everywhere.

Once, he nearly drowned there.

Another time, he saw a flying saucer
coming right at him!

He never got a chance to finish his pie,
because something would scare him every time.

And when Lawrence got scared,
he snapped into a ball and rolled away.

He would roll and bump, and roll and bump, down the hill toward home.

He hated it.

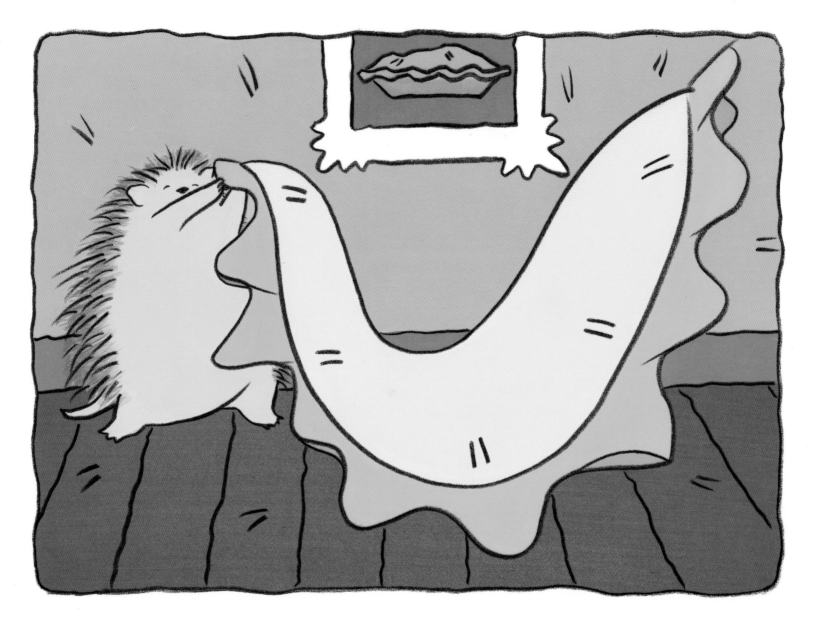

So today, to keep his mind off of pie,
Lawrence busied himself with chores at home.

It didn't help. He thought about pie the whole time.

Even at dinnertime . . .

. . . his cheese only made him think of pie.

He had missed out on so *much*
delicious coconut cream pie!

Lawrence was not going to miss out on any more!

It wasn't very far to the Grand Cafe.

Everything seemed quite calm there.

"I would like a large, gigantic, enormous piece of your best coconut cream pie," said Lawrence. "Please."

And then it came.

And it was so wonderfully delicious . . .

. . . that Lawrence didn't see a thing except
the pie slowly disappearing from his plate.

for Emily, Erin, Tiia, Peter, Sean,
Graham, Kristina, Evan, and Cameron

Published in the United States by
Dutton Children's Books,
a division of Penguin Books USA Inc.

Published simultaneously in Canada by
Fitzhenry & Whiteside Limited, Toronto

Designer: Barbara Powderly

Printed in Hong Kong by South China Printing Co.
First Edition   10 9 8 7 6 5 4 3 2 1

Library of Congress Cataloging-in-Publication Data

Stoeke, Janet Morgan.
    Lawrence/by Janet Morgan Stoeke.—1st ed.
        p. cm.
    Summary: A hedgehog with a love of coconut
cream pie overcomes his fears and goes to the
Grand Cafe to order a piece.
    ISBN 0-525-44602-8
    [1. Hedgehogs—Fiction.] I. Title.   89-38568
PZ7.S8696Law 1990   CIP
[E]—dc20   AC

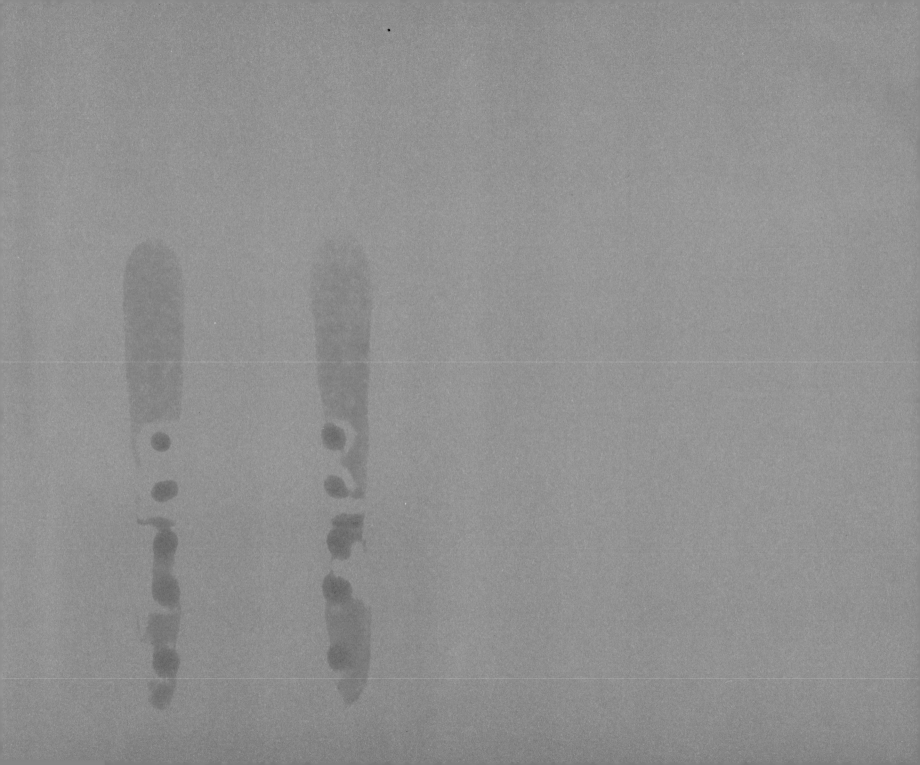